"Pet Care" Kids

CHARACTERS

Narrator 1	Cole
Narrator 2	Jade
Preston	Erica
Sandi	Mrs. Nielson
Mr. Drake	

SETTING

A typical neighborhood

Narrator 1: Young Preston Drake and his little sister Sandi had wanted a dog for months.

Narrator 2: They had asked their dad several times for a puppy. But he had said no every time.

Narrator 1: This time Mr. Preston decided to try something new.

Preston: Please, Dad. I promise to take care of him.

Sandi: And I'll help, too.

Mr. Drake: Well, I admit that I feel bad every time I tell you no. So I'm not going to say no now.

Preston: Really? Oh, wow! I'm going to get a dog.

Sandi: Me, too! Me, too!

Mr. Drake: Wait. Wait. Wait. I'm still not going to buy a dog for you.

Preston: But you said…

Mr. Drake: Just listen to me, OK?

Preston: OK. We'll listen.

Mr. Drake: You can have a dog if you take full responsibility for it. That means you have to pay for the dog and its license, vet visits, and supplies. You have to clean up after it. And when we go on vacations, you have to find a dog-sitter and pay him or her. Do you understand what I'm telling you?

Preston: I understand. How much will all that cost?

Mr. Drake: It depends on the dog you pick.

Preston: I've always wanted a golden retriever.

Sandi: I want a poodle.

Mr. Drake: You two will have to work that out. Then you'll need to find out how much your dog will cost. When you've earned the money, let me know.

Preston and **Sandi:** OK.

Narrator 2: Preston and Sandi were confused. They were happy that their dad had not said no.

Narrator 1: But they were upset that they would have to earn a lot of money.

Preston: Sandi, let's go outside. I need to think.

Sandi: OK. We can get the gold treever, Preston.

Preston: Golden retriever, Sandi. Thanks, but now I don't know if I still want one. It will be so much work.

Sandi: We don't know how much it will cost.

Narrator 1: Preston's best friend, Cole, came riding by on his bike.

Cole: Hey, Preston. What's the matter?

Sandi: He's sad.

Preston: It's complicated.

Cole: Why?

Preston: I want a dog.

Cole: Who doesn't know that?

Narrator 1: Their friends Erica and Jade were walking down the street. They stopped to talk.

Jade and **Erica:** Hi, guys.

Cole: Hi.

Jade: What are you doing?

Erica: What's the matter, Preston? You look sad.

Cole: It's something complicated. He was just about to tell me.

Jade: Can we help?

Sandi: Maybe.

Cole: Just tell us what it is.

Preston: OK. I want a dog.

Cole: Yeah, we all know that part.

Preston: And every time I've asked for one, my dad has said no. But this time he said yes.

Erica: That sounds great.

Sandi: Wait. He's not done.

Preston: I can have a dog, but I have to find out how much it costs and where to go to get one.

Cole: What's so bad about that?

Preston: I have to earn the money to pay for the dog, the vet visits, and all the supplies.

Jade: Yikes!

Preston: I know. That's why I feel bad.

Cole: Hey, I'm getting a weird feeling in my head. I think it's an idea.

Jade: Cool. What's your idea?

Cole: Let's start a business and earn the money.

Erica: We could buy a neighborhood dog. That would be great. It could stay at your house, but we'd all get to play with it when we want. OK?

Preston: It sounds OK.

Jade: How about a lemonade stand?

Preston: I don't think I want to sell lemonade every day.

Sandi: Let's walk all the dogs in the neighborhood. It might give us the feeling of having our own dog.

Preston: Sandi, that's a great idea.

Erica: This is going to be fun.

7

Narrator 2: The friends got together every day to plan their new business.

Narrator 1: First they decided to make flyers.

Jade: I love to draw. I can draw a picture of one of us walking a dog.

Erica: I'll use the computer to type the words.

Preston: How many flyers should we make? I can make copies at the grocery store.

Cole: I rode my bike around the neighborhood yesterday. There are 150 houses.

Preston: Let's see. Copies cost ten cents each. How much do we need to make copies for all the houses? I might have to ask my dad for a loan.

Cole: Math is my thing, guys. Ten cents times 150 copies equals, uh... fifteen dollars.

Preston: I have five dollars in my drawer.

Sandi: I have five dollars, too. That means we have ten dollars already.

Preston: Then we have to borrow only five more. I'll go talk to Dad.

Narrator 2: Preston went to talk to his dad. Jade and Erica went to Erica's house to make the flyers.

Preston: Dad, can I borrow five dollars? I'll pay you back.

Mr. Drake: What do you need the money for?

Preston: Sandi and I and our friends are starting a pet-care business. We want to earn money to buy our new dog. We have to make advertising flyers.

Mr. Drake: That sounds good, but when banks make business loans, they charge interest.

Preston: What does that mean?

Mr. Drake: It means you have to pay to borrow the money. The longer you borrow the money, the more you have to pay.

Preston: Oh, I see. Is the interest a lot?

Mr. Drake: You can have the five-dollar loan at an interest rate of ten cents per week. The first week will be free. If you pay me back by the end of the first week, I won't charge you the ten cents.

Preston: That seems fair.

Narrator 1: The next day the friends got together after school. Preston had the fifteen dollars. Jade and Erica had the flyers.

Cole: Those flyers look great. We'll make tons of money.

Narrator 2: The flyers said:

All: "Pet Care" Kids: We take care of your pet's needs. We walk dogs, feed them, and give them baths. We pick up after them, too. We puppy-sit when you go somewhere. Cats, birds, and fish welcome. Call us."

Narrator 1: The prices were listed on the flyer.

Jade: Dog-walking—one dollar.

Cole: Dog-feeding—fifty cents.

Sandi: Dog baths—two dollars for small dogs.

Preston: Four dollars for big dogs.

Erica: Puppy-sitting—time-dependent. Call us!

Narrator 2: They listed Jade's phone number. Jade had allergies, so she couldn't work with the animals. But she could answer the phones.

Narrator 1: Preston, Sandi, and Cole went to make the copies.

Narrator 2: The next day the friends passed out the flyers. Then they waited.

Narrator 1: Days went by with no phone calls. They began to worry.

Preston: Still no calls? I have to pay Dad ten cents every week in interest starting Monday.

Erica: And we still haven't made any money for buying your dog.

Sandi: This is hard!

Narrator 1: The next day, Jade arrived at the meeting with good news.

Jade: I answered three calls yesterday.

Sandi: Neat-o!

Jade: The first job is for Cole. Saturday, Mr. Lester wants you to give Griz, his Yorkie, a bath.

Cole: I'll do it. That's two dollars.

Jade: Erica, you need to kitty-sit for Mr. and Mrs. Norman. They have that fluffy white kitty named Jazzy. They are going on vacation for a week. She will give you twenty dollars if you water her plants and feed Jazzy.

Erica: That's a lot of money! But we won't get it until next week. We still can't pay Mr. Drake.

Jade: Wait. Preston and Sandi, you're going to walk Mrs. Nielson's golden retriever, Lady, starting tomorrow after school. If Lady likes you, you are hired for weekdays. You'll get weekends off.

Sandi: Neat-o! But today is Wednesday. That leaves only Thursday and Friday.

Preston: That's two dollars more. Oh well, we'll just have to pay Dad the dime in interest. At least we're making money.

Narrator 2: Everyone did their assigned jobs.

Narrator 1: Cole got another dog-bath job on Saturday. The owner paid Cole an extra dollar for doing a good job with his St. Bernard.

Narrator 2: The next Saturday afternoon, the group got together again.

Sandi: How much do we have now?

Preston: Well, we have the twenty dollars from Erica's job. We made one dollar for each of the seven days of dog-walking.

Cole: And I brought in seven dollars for doggie baths. So in a week and a half, we made, uh.... thirty-four dollars. Wow!

Preston: Don't forget to subtract five dollars and ten cents.

Cole: That leaves…

All kids: Twenty-eight dollars and ninety cents.

Jade: That's great. We'll have enough to buy a neighborhood dog in no time at all.

Preston: Remember, we have to make enough money for all the related costs.

Narrator 1: It took exactly 10 weeks to save the money. It was time to buy a neighborhood dog.

Narrator 2: But then plans changed a bit.

Narrator 1: Sandi and Preston kept going to Mrs. Nielson's house to walk Lady. But on this Monday, Lady wasn't at the door like she usually was.

Mrs. Nielson: Lady isn't going on a walk today. She's in her doggie bed.

Narrator 2: The kids went to see Lady. They could hear funny squeaking sounds. There next to Lady were four golden retriever puppies.

Sandi: Puppies! Oh, look how little they are.

Preston: What are you going to do with them when they're grown, Mrs. Nielson?

Mrs. Nielson: In about six weeks, these puppies will need a new home. You don't happen to know anyone who wants a new golden retriever, do you?

Preston: I would love one. How much is one?

Mrs. Nielson: For you and Sandi, it's free. I know you'll give your puppy a good home.

Sandi: Not just a good home, a neighborhood. We have three partners who will share our new puppy.

Mrs. Nielson: You children have done a great job. Congratulations on your new dog and on your business success!

The End